of a

FAIRYTALE
VILLAIN

CONFESSIONS
of a
FAIRYTALE
VILLAIN

Cinderella's not so ugly sister

Claire Pyatt

Illustrated by Bee Willey

Potter Books

Written by Claire Pyatt
Designed by Tracey Cunnell
and Kevin Knight
Edited by Pat Hegarty
Additional material written by Helen Keith
Illustrated by Bee Willey

Illustrations copyright © 2009 Bee Willey
Cover background © iStockphoto
Page decorations © iStockphoto

Created by WizzBook Ltd
Copyright © 2009 WizzBook Ltd
All rights reserved.

First published in the UK
by Potter Books, RH17 5PA, UK

www.potterbooks.co.uk

Printed in China

Me (Mildred)

This is Mildred's very
own PRIVATE AND
PERSONAL diary – KEEP OUT!
(Yes, I DO mean you, Agatha.)

Mum
(The Wicked
Stepmother)

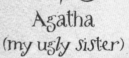

Agatha
(my ugly sister)

Bo Peep
(my best friend)

Josh
x x x

AUGUST

August 10th

Cinderella moved the last of her stuff out today.
Not that she had much, just a couple of carrier
bags of belongings and her scruffy old dog. Felt
a bit bad actually. I'm going to miss her, and not
just because she did all the housework; I used to
quite like talking to her, and didn't really enjoy
being mean to her all that much. Better not tell
Mum and Agatha though. They're still fuming over
the fact that she was the only one of us who had
feet small enough for the glass slipper.

Really, am secretly pleased it didn't fit me.
Didn't think it looked very comfortable.

Watched Cinderella from the window, getting
into her golden coach – felt quite jealous. Maybe

if I'd been a bit nicer to her when she lived here she would have let me have a ride in it.

August 15th

It's not even been a week and the house is already a tip. We don't have any clean clothes and none of us can cook so we've had takeaways every night. I shoved the pizza boxes under the sofa last night to make it look a bit tidier, and I saw the strangest thing. I know this sounds crazy, but I'm sure I saw a little mouse wearing a hat and a T-shirt. Think I must have eaten too many additives and it's affected my brain. Went to tell Mum and Agatha about it but they were whispering in the kitchen, huddled over a book. They both looked guilty when I came in and Mum quickly put the book in a drawer. Maybe they're planning a surprise birthday party for me (very, very far in advance). Ooh, feel quite excited.

August 16th

Snuck downstairs last night once everyone was asleep and looked in the drawer. Was hoping to find a party planning guide or something, but was just a boring old spell book. Wonder what they're doing with that? They've never bothered with magic before – just being mean seemed to get them their own way.

August 21st

Things are getting worse! Not sure how much more fast food and beans on toast I can take, plus am wearing a dress that Cinderella wouldn't have scrubbed the hearth with. Really wish I had asked her how to work the washing machine before she left. And the vacuum cleaner. And the dishwasher.

After lunch, Mum found me squirting washing-up liquid on to the plates that I had stacked neatly in the machine. She wanted to know what on earth I was doing. I was thinking the same thing myself. Had just thought it would be nice to eat off a clean plate. Not sure I did it right – threw in a bucket of water and slammed it shut. Still ended up washing the plates by hand because I really couldn't work out how to get the dishwasher going.

Mum not impressed with my next comment.

Wondered out loud if I should just call Cinderella and ask her how everything works. I was met with a cold silence. Mum says she doesn't want to hear 'that ungrateful wretch' mentioned in this house. Will keep quiet from now on.

Felt surprisingly good to be doing something for myself for a change. Wish I'd done it ages ago.

August 22nd

Tidied my room today, it looks much better. Just wish I could get the vacuum working. Used a dustpan and brush to sweep up the worst of it, which did the trick. Went to bed exhausted. Didn't realise housework was such, well, work. No wonder Cinderella used to look so sad about having to do it all the time. Think I'll give her a call tomorrow.

August 23rd

Hung around downstairs for ages trying to get the phone to myself. Agatha got v. suspicious. Said I was waiting for a call and wondered if it would be okay to keep the phone in my room for a while.

I didn't want her to know that I was waiting for her and Mum to clear off long enough for me to call Cinderella. Mum will go mad if she finds out.

Agatha's so mean. She just sneered and said who would ever call me. She said it's not like I've got any friends or anything, and no boys are ever likely to ask for my number. Sad thing is, she's right. Also said she wouldn't recommend taking the phone upstairs because Mum was waiting for a call from the fruiterer. What's that all about?

Thought about what she said. We've never had any friends. I suppose that's what happens when your mum becomes a Wicked Stepmother. She's right about boyfriends too. Although, I did kiss Georgie Porgie once (apparently he's not fussy), but he cried. Everyone said it was a first.

August 25th

I never got a chance to call Cinderella in the end. The fruiterer rang and Mum was on the phone to him for about an hour and a half. Anyway, it doesn't matter because this morning a letter arrived from the palace! I got to the door first when the post arrived (not too difficult since Mum and Agatha sleep in until at least noon), and was surprised to find a scroll bearing the royal seal amongst the bills and Mum's copy of Poisoners' Weekly (what's she subscribing to that for?). My hands were shaking with excitement as I read it:

Dear Lady Fontaine and her daughters,
Agatha and Mildred,

Miss Cinderella Fontaine and
HRH The Handsome Prince
request the pleasure of your company at the palace
on September 16th at 7pm to celebrate their engagement.

Dinner and dancing will be followed by
entertainment provided by Snow White
and her band, The Seven Dwarves.

(Ball gowns and glass slippers are preferred but not essential)

RSVP

Cinderella and The Handsome Prince

I can't believe it, a party! I've spent years
wishing I would get invited to parties and now,
two in a month; first the Prince's ball at the palace
(admittedly, that could have turned out better),
and now this. I can't wait to go shopping for a
new dress. Not sure about the whole glass slippers
thing though. Apart from being uncomfortable
(I bet I can't even walk in them) they're bound
to be really expensive. We can't all have Fairy
Godmothers, can we? Cinderella really should
have thought about that.

August 27th

Still haven't told Mum and Agatha about the letter
from the palace; bit worried about the effect it will
have on them, to be honest. Well, Mum's told me
not to even mention Cinders' name, and Agatha
is inconsolable. She keeps wailing that it should
have been her and only stops crying when she
finds a Justin Timberlake video on MTV.

Mum is still angry that it wasn't me or Agatha
who managed to bag the Prince. She says we
weren't trying hard enough. She might be right on

my part – have never really thought all that much of The Handsome Prince. He's a bit too handsome, if you know what I mean. I bet Cinderella can't get into the bathroom in the mornings because he's in front of the mirror for so long. And a girl shouldn't have to share her straighteners with her boyf – it's just wrong.

August 28th

I sent off a little note to the palace this morning telling Cinderella that Mum and Agatha both have a cold (they have huge noses, so they always have colds for ages), but that I'd love to come. There doesn't seem to be much point in telling them about the party. They won't want to go, and if they know about it then I won't be able to go either. I think the best thing is just to sneak out. They probably won't even notice I'm gone. They're both acting very strangely these days; they were in the kitchen all afternoon and wouldn't let me in. There were some very strange smells coming from in there, too. Maybe it's all the takeaways starting to affect their digestion, if you know what I mean.

August 29th

Went into town today to find a dress to wear
to Cinderella's party, but it didn't exactly go as
planned. I walked past Princesses' Tresses, the
trendy new hair place in the high street, just as
Goldilocks and Rapunzel came out (can't believe
how quickly Rapunzel's hair has grown back after
that witch cut it off). At first I thought they hadn't
seen me but they had, and flounced over, wafting
smells of shampoo.

Rapunzel smiled – at first I checked behind
me but there was no one else she could've been
looking at. 'Hey, love your shoes!' she said.

Dur, I smiled and said thanks. How wrong could
I be? I guess my scruffy baseball pumps aren't her
idea of stylish. They both shrieked with laughter
and clattered off on their sparkly heels, waving their
carrier bags of conditioning treatment samples.

Stupid airheads – especially that Rapunzel. She's
just jealous because my stepsister is marrying The
Handsome Prince and he used to climb up her hair.
Well, I don't think it's too clever to have hair that
long. I bet her split ends are dreadful. And she must

spend a fortune on shampoo.

Thinking about it, Goldilocks isn't really one to judge either, not with her criminal record. I didn't even know what breaking and entering was until I read about her in the papers – and she was done for damage to property and theft. Not as squeaky clean as she'd like you to think, huh?

Luckily, there was no one around to witness my humiliation so I carried on to The Ball Gown Emporium. Found a gorgeous blue dress that the assistant said brought out my eyes. Think she might have been working on commission, because when I held it up to me and looked in the mirror I couldn't see what she was talking about. Still, the colour did take the focus off my nose, which can only be a good thing. Just as I was about to try it on, Sleeping Beauty came in with one of her maids-in-waiting (who was carrying pillows and a duvet, just in case), and I ended up putting the dress back on the rack before scurrying out.

Why does the prettiest girl in town always walk in to the communal changing room when you're just about to try something on?

August 30th

Still feeling deflated after yesterday, am really wishing that I'd just tried that dress on.

Shouldn't feel intimidated by all these princess types with their phenomenal hair and fashion sense, and especially not by Sleeping Beauty. She probably wouldn't have stayed awake long enough to see me try the dress on anyway.

'What's up with you?' asked Agatha this morning. She was lounging on my bed, still in her pyjamas, watching me tie my hair up in the mirror. (Instead of moaning about my big nose and feet and the gap between my front teeth, I'm only focusing on the positives. I've decided that I like my hair. Sure, it's not a silken blonde curtain like a lot of girls around here, but it is long and I quite like the colour; a sort of chocolate brown. At least it's different – and it's super shiny.) 'I said, what's up with you?' she asked again, impatiently.

Told her I just thought I'd try something different with my hair, that's all. Her answer? 'Why bother?' That seems to be her answer to everything. Mind you, it used to be mine too.

I'm glad I've decided to start bothering about things like that.

Just after lunch the doorbell went while we were all lazing on the sofa. Mum and Agatha ignored it.

The doorbell went again, but Mum just turned up the TV so I got up to get it. Had to step over hundreds of empty crisp packets and burger boxes. Is just getting ridiculous now. I did start picking it all up and sorting it for the recycling, but no one helped me so now I just do my own. I feel so guilty when I think of all the times I would get Cinderella to clear up after me. After the way we treated her, it's no wonder she couldn't wait to leave. I am definitely going to apologise when I see her at the party. Was pretty decent of her to invite us, come to think of it.

I opened the door to Little Bo Peep, who was weeping on the doorstep. There was no need for me to ask her what was wrong; it's always the same thing.

'I'm sorry to bother you, Mildred,' she sniffed. 'But I've lost my sheep and I...'

'Don't know where to find them?' I finished for her and she nodded and sniffed, wiping her nose on the back of her lace-gloved hand. Honestly, this is the fourth time this month. I don't know why she doesn't fit her bloomin' sheep with some sort of tracking device and be done with it.

Agatha came up behind me and slammed the door shut in Bo Peep's face. I shot her a look and ran out after Bo Peep, who was already halfway up the path. I could hear Agatha and Mum saying that I was soft in the head, but I didn't care. I offered to help Bo Peep look for her sheep. We looked everywhere, it was a total 'mare. Was just asking Jack and Jill if we could go to the top of their hill to see if we could spot the sheep from up there, when Mary came storming over to us. She was bright red in the face and sooooooo cross. She yelled at Bo Peep that her stupid sheep had got into the pen with her Little Lamb and were chasing him all over the place.

Took us about two hours to round them all up. Bo Peep was so grateful. We sat down in an exhausted heap and she said thanks – and she called me Milly! She said it normally takes much longer than that when she's on her own, and that no one ever wants to help. Thought she was going to burst into tears, and then she said I was a real friend for helping!

Could hardly believe what I was hearing. A friend? And Milly? Why have I never thought of calling myself that before? It's so much prettier than Mildred. Could hardly stop grinning.

Spent rest of the afternoon chatting to Bo Peep. She's really lovely despite being totally rubbish at the sheep thing.

Mum was furious when I got home. Demanded to know where I'd been, as soon as I got through the door. She wasn't impressed when I told her. She said that if I start doing favours for people then they'll come to expect it, and will take advantage of me. Said I should follow my sister's example.

Glorious sister in question was lying on the sofa – still. She hadn't even got dressed. She looked up at me and snorted horribly, then turned back to the TV. 'Complete waste of time, making friends,' she said, grumpily.

Don't care what they say, it feels great to have done something nice for someone.

August 31st

Am adding 'clear skin' to my list of Things I Like About Me. It's positively glowing this morning. Also, am going to start asking people to call me Milly – I love it. Ha, I noticed that wart on the end of Agatha's nose is getting bigger and hairier! Not that she seems to care; she's too busy whispering in corners with Mum.

They're definitely up to something.

SEPTEMBER

September 5th

Mum has finally decided to do something about
the state of the house; she's interviewing cleaners
tomorrow. It's about time. The living room looks
like a landfill site. Forget that mouse I thought I
saw – we've probably got rats by now.

Have been trying to listen in on Mum and
Agatha's secret little chats, but still haven't
worked out what's going on. A man from the
market turned up here yesterday with 'apple
samples' and the three of them were holed up
in the kitchen for most of the morning. When
they finally came out, I asked Agatha what they
were doing in there. She said that her and Mum
were going to bake a pie. They both collapsed into

fits of laughter. Don't see what's so funny myself.
Must be a private joke.

September 6th

The first interviewee arrived at 9 o'clock. I was
surprised to see Mum and my sister up so early, and
dressed so smartly too. I showed Little Miss Muffet
into the study (it's the only room that isn't carpeted
in dirty plates and food wrappers) and went to get
her a drink. When I came back in, she was telling
Mum about the three years that she worked as a
cleaner for The Seven Dwarves, before Snow White
moved in and she was made redundant.

Apparently, the Dwarves have begged her to go
back; she thinks they're struggling now that Snow
White has moved in with Prince Charming. She got
all huffy and said she can't just forget how they
dropped her as soon as they had someone else.
Mind you, as she was getting into a bit of a rant
about this, I noticed her checking out our house.
Her eyes roamed around the room and I think
she noticed the huge number of cobwebs floating
across the ceiling. Maybe that's what did it...

Little Miss Muffet turned a weird colour and got warily to her feet. She kept backing away from her chair and said that on second thoughts, she wasn't sure this job was for her. She muttered something about getting into law or teaching and then rushed out of the room without even finishing her coffee. Ho hum.

The other interviews were no better; the applicants were either past it (Old Mother Hubbard), or too young (Little Boy Blue). Mum had just about given up when Mary-Mary arrived. After a bit of small talk about how well her garden is growing, and the silver bells looking beautiful at this time of year, Mum seemed quite impressed. Mary-Mary isn't half as contrary as she is made out to be. In fact, Mum offered her the job on the spot. Mary-Mary accepted and has agreed to do the garden as well.

September 10th

Mary-Mary has only been working here for three days and already Mum and Agatha are ordering her about like they used to do with Cinderella.

I've made a promise to myself that I won't act like that again, and so I've told Mary-Mary that I'll clean my room and do my own washing. I've actually really enjoyed doing it. Don't think that Mary-Mary will put up with being bossed about for long though; she told me that she only really wanted the job because our garden is so huge and she had some great ideas for it, and also that if Agatha asks her for a drink again without saying 'please', then she's going to put a bogey in it. Not sure if she was joking or not. Have made a mental note to always remember to say please and thank you, just in case.

September 11th

Was surprised to get a phone call from Bo Peep this morning. Thought at first she needed help looking for her sheep again, but she didn't (Old MacDonald was watching them for her), she wanted me to meet her in town tomorrow.

Wasn't sure I'd heard her right. Can't remember the last time someone wanted me to meet them in town. Or anywhere else for that matter. But she seemed to mean it – she even said we could look for an outfit for me to wear to Cinders' party – so we're meeting at twelve outside The Spell Shop.

I'm worried that I sounded far too keen. Don't want her to think I'm a sad loner, desperate for friends. Actually I don't care. Now, what am I going to wear?

September 12th

Was up by six this morning. Stood in front of my open wardrobe for about the next hour and mentally rejected every outfit I own. After my shower I returned to the wardrobe, hoping that the perfect outfit had suddenly materialised. It hadn't. Wished I had a Fairy Godmother. Or some woodland creature friends; those little birds and mice can rustle up a dress, no problem.

Settled for jeans but felt seriously underdressed. Was nervous about meeting Bo Peep, thought she was bound to own masses of amazing princess-type outfits to wear. Also had serious doubts as to whether she would actually turn up, so was surprised to find that she was already there when I arrived, and not a puff sleeve in sight.

Got off to a good start – Bo Peep even linked arms with me and asked if I wanted to try The Ball Gown Emporium first. I confessed about my last trip there, and why I hadn't tried the dress on. She was really sweet, and said I shouldn't have taken any notice of Sleeping Beauty. Big gossip: apparently those movie-star looks are thanks to a scalpel rather than good genes or the gift of a Good Fairy! No way!

This time I was bold and I tried the dress on. Bo Peep said it was gorgeous; I'm sure she said I looked beautiful. I really loved the dress – and I love it when Bo Peep calls me Milly. Makes me feel like a different person. (In fact, have told Mum and Agatha that I want them to call me that. Of course, they laughed at me. Mum says Milly's a pretty girl's name. Am going to rise above such comments from now on.)

The dress was in the sale, so I could afford shoes too. Went to The Shoemaker's and got his elves to make me some. They were fab; the same shade of blue as the dress with the perfect amount of sparkle. We stopped off at Bo's house on the

way back (that's what I call her now) and she
lent me a beautiful necklace and some earrings.
Couldn't wait to get home to try them on with the
dress. Spent most of the evening admiring myself
in my bedroom mirror, then had to quickly shove it
all under the bed when I heard Agatha coming.

Good job I did, as she just barged in without
knocking. Kept thinking about my poor dress all
bundled up on the floor and imagined how creased
it must be. Got the inquisition from Agatha –
where had I been all day, who with, doing what?
Just told her that Bo Peep and I had been in town.
Then Agatha gasped, 'Where did you get those?'

Pudding and pie! Had forgotten to take the
earrings out and typical eagle-eyes Agatha had
spotted them. Tried to sound casual and said I'd
had them for ages, but I could feel my cheeks
grow red hot. Should've just said that I'd bought
them today.

Of course, Agatha didn't believe me. Should've
known – she's 'borrowed' stuff from my jewellery
box loads of times, she would have remembered
them. (By 'borrowed' I mean 'taken without asking

and then not bothered to put back'.) Then guess what she said? 'You didn't steal them, did you?' Trust her to think of that. Had to give in and tell her that Bo Peep had lent them to me – so then of course all I got was abuse about having a new friend. According to the mean-spirited Agatha, it's because I'm the only person round here who's stupid enough to help Bo Peep look for her 'idiot sheep' every five minutes.

Not listening to her. She's just jealous. Hope she's not right.

September 14th

Went to Bo's house and we tried a few things out with my hair; think I'm going to have it up for the party. Have always avoided that in the past because it shows how much my ears stick out. Turns out they don't look as bad as I thought.

The sheep had escaped from their pen – again – and it took us a while to round them up. By the time I got home it was quite late and I was sure that Mum would be angry that I'd missed tea, but when I got in the house was quiet. Mum and Agatha were sitting at the kitchen table with a hideous-looking old woman dressed in a black cloak. They all stopped talking when I walked in and stared at me. Mumbled my apologies and backed straight back out again. Have been lying awake for ages thinking about the creepy old woman in our kitchen. I'm sure I've seen her somewhere before.

September 15th

I asked Agatha this morning who that woman was last night. 'None of your business,' she snorted, squeezing her spots in the mirror. (Can't remember the last time I had a blemish on my skin. It's really strange.)

She says the woman is just a friend of hers and Mum's. Then sneered, 'Or are you the only one who's allowed to have friends?'

Really hate her right now.

September 15th (later)

I'm going to a party tomorrow night!!!!
SOOOOOOO excited!

September 16th

Was the most amazing night! Told Mum I was
sleeping over at Bo Peep's so that I could get ready
at her house. Thought I'd be faced with a squillion
questions but she seemed quite glad to get rid of
me for the evening.

Bo said I looked really beautiful once I was
in my dress with my hair and make-up all done.
Have never attempted to put make-up on before
– never been sure how – but Bo did a really good
job. I could honestly say, for the first time ever,
that I did look pretty.

Cinderella was open-mouthed when she saw
me. Said she almost didn't recognise me, and kept
saying wow! That made me so happy. I gave her a
big hug and told her I like to be called Milly now.
She seemed to like it, too.

It was so nice to catch up with my stepsister.
Told her about Mary-Mary working at ours, and
how I've become friends with Bo Peep. Cinders
seemed dead chuffed for me. She asked if Mum
and Aggie were feeling better.

Forgot that I'd told her they'd been ill.

Said they were still moaning and sniffing all the time. Cinderella frowned, then said, 'Mum sounded fine when I spoke to her on the phone.' AAAAGH!

My heart was pounding in my chest. Did Mum know I was at the party?

I quizzed her about when they'd spoken, and what about. Cinders told me that Mum and Agatha have offered to do the food for the wedding. Huh?!

Was whisked off to meet everyone else. Got a bit confused with all the princes: there was The Handsome Prince of course, plus Snow White's husband Prince Charming and Sleeping Beauty's husband The Prince. Then I was introduced to All The King's Men and The Seven Dwarves, so by the time dinner was served my head was swimming with names. Sat next to Snow White's cousin, Rose Red, a girl who totally knows what it's like to live in the shadow of a far more beautiful relative.

When I told her that I was Cinderella's stepsister she seemed quite shocked. Said she

was expecting an Ugly Sister, from what she'd read in the papers. 'Just goes to show you can't believe everything you read, doesn't it?' she said, shovelling in a forkful of risotto. Thought I was going to burst with joy.

Can't even begin to describe the party. It was just amazing. Danced pretty much all night, without even feeling stupid or self-conscious. The time just flew by – good job Cinderella's parties carry on past midnight these days.

Cinderella hugged me when I left and told me again how lovely I looked and that Snow White and Sleeping Beauty hadn't even recognised me! We agreed to see each other soon – and then, thank goodness, she promised that she hadn't told Mum that I was coming tonight.

Got home seriously late, but managed to sneak in without waking anyone and went straight to the kitchen to make myself a mug of hot chocolate. Moved a huge pile of cookery books out of the way and a piece of paper fluttered to the ground. Picked it up and read it, don't know if that's bad?

WEDDING DESSERTS

Apple pie

Apple tart

Apple and cinnamon bake

Apple surprise!!!!

Maybe Mum and Agatha have turned over a new leaf and are helping out with Cinderella's wedding out of the goodness of their hearts? Maybe even they are actually getting bored of doing nothing all day? Sincerely doubt it.

September 17th

Had a lovely lazy day. Feet are killing me after
all that dancing last night, but don't care. Keep
reliving it all and am walking around with a
dreamy smile on my face. Had to laugh – Agatha
was trying to wind me up by saying I was grinning
like an idiot, and looked just like Cinderella. That's
not an insult in my book, but I'm sure Agatha
meant it as one.

September 21st

That weird old woman came round again today.
Mum said she's helping her out with some recipes.
Plucked up the courage to ask if it's true that
she has volunteered to do the food for the
wedding. She said that it was going to be her
wedding present. Am finding it very hard to
believe that, after all the yelling, wringing of
hands and chucking around of crockery after
the glass slipper episode, not only has she
accepted the wedding, but has actually
volunteered to cater for it. It's not even like
she can cook.

September 25th

On the doormat this morning was Mum's latest copy of Poisoners' Weekly. Did a double take when I saw the front cover – featuring the old woman who was in our house last week! I knew I recognised her; she's The Wicked Queen, famous for disguising herself as an old woman and sneaking into the Big Brother house with poisoned apples. She's been coming round to 'help' Mum and Agatha with 'recipes' for the wedding.

I think Cinderella may be in trouble.

October

October 1st

Have spent the last five days carefully thinking over all the evidence:

- Mum and Agatha's secretive behaviour
- Spell book in the kitchen
- Calls and visits from the fruiterer – apples
- Poisoners' Weekly
- Creepy old woman aka Wicked Queen
- Offering to do food for Cinderella's wedding

Mum and Agatha are planning to poison Cinderella on her wedding day!!!!

Don't want to believe that they would seriously consider something like that, but what other explanation is there? Exactly. It's at times like this that I realise how much need there is for some sort of law enforcement around here. I'm sure there wouldn't be half the attempted murders, blowing down of houses, and locking up of princesses by wicked witches if there was.

October 3rd

As far as I can see I have three options:

<u>Confront Mum and Agatha</u> – far too dangerous. Won't be able to help anyone if they do away with me too.

<u>Tell Cinderella</u> – seems a bit cruel. Am sure she has enough to worry about with planning a wedding, let alone the added stress of an assassination attempt.

<u>Stop them myself</u> – not too thrilled about this idea to be honest, especially as I have absolutely no idea how to do it. Needs some thinking time.

October 5th

Okay. Have had a few ideas, but will need some help. Tried to call Bo so I could discuss it with her, but there was no answer. When I went to her house her mum said she was out looking for her sheep. Big surprise.

The smell of apple pie wafting down the path to greet me when I got back home would normally have made my mouth water. This time it made me feel sick. Practically ran past the kitchen to get upstairs to my room, and nearly knocked Mary-Mary flying as she was coming down with an armful of Agatha's dirty washing.

Tried to force a smile, but Mary-Mary could tell something was wrong. She was really kind and I was terrified I was going to start crying and blurt it all out to her. Just shook my head and told her it was the smell of the pies – said it was making me really hungry and I was supposed to be cutting out puddings. Then, to make things worse, Mary-Mary started going on about seeing Mum and Agatha in a whole new light, making this wonderful gesture for Cinderella.

She should have been called Mary-Mary Quite Gullible.

Finally got hold of Bo really late tonight. Tried to tell her about the poison in the apple pies, but she just kept yawning and asking what I was going on about. Was scared stiff that Mum or Agatha might hear me. Realised that I wasn't getting much sense out of Bo, so persuaded her to meet me by the fountain at 9am tomorrow.

After several minutes of moaning about tomorrow being a Sunday and 9am being far too early, she finally agreed. Am actually a bit annoyed that she couldn't understand the urgency of this situation.

October 6th

Lay awake for hours until the sun came up, then finally felt myself drifting off around 6am. Was woken an hour later by Bo frantically banging on the front door.

Screwed my eyes up against the sunshine and felt a bit peeved that meeting me at 9am had been met with such opposition, yet banging on the door and waking me up at 7am was perfectly acceptable. Bo was in a right tizzy, though. She urged me to get dressed, while telling me that All The King's Horses and All The King's Men had just galloped through the village.

Wasn't sure of the importance of this, but Bo insisted it must mean that something was going on – maybe an accident or something. Told her that's sick, but said I'd get dressed and be back down in a minute. Suggested she wait in the kitchen, but then had a panic and made her promise not to touch anything. Not sure what's poisoned and what isn't.

Bo rolled her eyes as she went into the kitchen. 'Do you seriously think that your mum and sister are going to try to poison Cinderella?' she asked when I came downstairs.

I really do. They've been baking pies all week but then throwing them out. I reckon they're having a bit of trouble getting the poison right or something. Bo thinks that's rubbish proof and it's more likely that they're just hopeless at cooking.

Told her about the subscription to the poisoning

magazine, the spell book and the visits from
The Wicked Queen. Bo wants to know why they
need The Wicked Queen if they've got a spell
book. Have already figured that one out: the
spell book is a new edition, the Sleeping Death
Potion was banned before it came out, so it's
not in there.

Bo also wants to know why they don't just
get The Wicked Queen to make the potion for
them. My best guess here is that they daren't
get her to make it, as she's banned from practising
magic. The Sorcerers' Council took away her
licence after the Big Brother shenanigans. But
she could teach Mum and Agatha how to do it
themselves. I think it's just taking them a while
because they have no natural ability (yes, that's
a polite way of saying that they're a bit thick,
as Bo pointed out).

Anyway, by the time we'd been through all this
we'd arrived in the village square. Bo was staring
open-mouthed at the commotion.

All The King's Men had dismounted and were
untying bundles of refuse sacks and spades.

Even though it was early, a small crowd had already gathered and some of The King's Men were trying to move them along. As they dispersed we could see that there, on the floor in front of the large stone wall, were the remains of a huge egg.

Bo clapped her hand to her mouth in horror. 'Humpty Dumpty!' she gasped. Large fragments of Humpty's shell were scattered as far as the foot of Jack and Jill's Hill, and the pool of yolk was spreading slowly across the entire square. 'I can't look,' she said, turning away. 'I think I'm going to be sick.'

October 7th

All The King's Horses and All The King's Men couldn't put Humpty together again, even though they worked long into the night. Floodlights were set up in the square once it got dark, but by morning reports were coming through that the repair mission had been abandoned and now they were mounting a clean-up operation. Sat up all night watching the news and woke up on the sofa. Agatha was beside me eating a bowl of cereal.

'Don't know what all the fuss is about,' she snorted, spraying the TV screen with a shower of cornflakes. 'That egg must have been about a hundred years old.'

Can't believe she doesn't think it's sad. Humpty Dumpty was the oldest resident of Storybook. All she said was she thinks it's sad that they're appealing for help to clear it all up. According to her, that's All The King's Men's job – that's what we pay taxes for. She's such a cow sometimes – and I don't mean she can jump over the moon. (Although I wish she would, and land far, far away.)

As I left the house I met Bo coming up the garden path. Asked if she wanted to go and help with the clean-up and she nodded – she was just coming to ask me that. Proves that we're meant to be friends, think we're on the same wavelength a lot of the time. Although, she did also ask if I could help her find the sheep first. Seems they got out AGAIN last night.

Was brave this time, and told her to leave them alone. Sure they'll come home by themselves – probably wagging their tails behind them.

Bo shrugged and decided it'd be worth a try. She held up a huge basket filled with sandwiches and bottles of lemonade for All The King's Men. Good thinking, that girl.

Was pleasantly surprised to see how many people had turned up to help: Jack and Jill were scooping up yolk with their pails, Little Miss Muffet and Mother Goose were sweeping broken egg shell into piles and The Three Little Pigs were shovelling the piles into sacks. Little Red Riding Hood was skipping around handing out muffins to the volunteers and All The King's Men. I looked at Bo's scowling face, and tried to reassure her – I bet LRRH didn't bring anything to drink. Said I thought the muffins looked very dry, too. Seemed to cheer her up.

Someone handed us brooms and we set to work and, as I'd predicted, Bo's lemonade was gratefully received. Goldilocks and Rapunzel were sitting on the wall, swinging their legs and flirting with All The King's Men – despite being warned several times how dangerous it was. Goldilocks kept flicking her hair, asking The King's Men if they'd catch her if she fell, and reapplying her lip gloss.

At one point she let go of the tube and it fell on to Bo's head. Bo handed it back, trying to smile through gritted teeth. Goldilocks just smiled and left it, saying Bo needs it more than she does. Grrrr.

Spent the rest of the day wishing that Goldilocks and Rapunzel really would fall off the wall.

October 10th

Day four of the clean-up. Have been coming home late and covered in sticky yolk every night this week. Mum and Agatha haven't even asked me where I've been, much less offered to help. They're still spending every spare moment in the kitchen. Tried to get in there yesterday evening so I could see what's going on, but they've put a lock on the door.

Bo still isn't convinced that a poisoning plot is afoot. She thinks I'm reading far too much into it, and even asked what hard evidence I've actually got.

Has she not listened to anything I've said? I heaved myself on to the wall and looked at her as if she were stupid. 'Er, the spell book, poisoning magazines, whispering behind closed doors, truckloads of apples being delivered every week, a woman who has previous form coming to the house every five minutes,' I said, counting the points off on my fingers.

That made her admit that it doesn't look good. But she's still saying that maybe they've just turned over a new leaf and want to do something nice for Cinders. She sounds just like Mary-Mary.

I'm telling you, they're up to no good. Still not sure what to do yet, so told Bo about the ideas I've had:

• Finding out the ingredients needed for the potion and swapping them for something identical looking, but harmless.
• Cancelling the order from the fruiterer (but if Mum calls fruiterer, they will know that it was down to me).
• Hiding their cookery books so that they can't even make the pies in the first place.

I admit these ideas aren't the best in the world. Firstly, they depend on me actually being able to get into the kitchen and secondly, they won't be easy to carry out on my own.

Bo didn't seem thrilled with the idea of helping me out. Like she says, assuming that I'm right and they are trying to poison Cinderella, what will they do to us if they catch us trying to stop them? They're clearly not mentally stable.

Then she thought she'd cracked it. What if we let them carry on with their plan, and when they ('if they', according to Bo) serve poisoned apple pie to Cinderella, we just get the spell broken by true love's kiss – from The Handsome Prince.

Nice idea, but there's one hitch. It's love's <u>first</u> kiss. And, like I pointed out, they'll already be married by the time they eat, so Cinders will have had her first kiss.

Jumped out of our skins – and nearly fell off the wall ourselves – when we heard a voice behind us. 'This sounds like an interesting conversation!'

Turning round, I saw one of The King's Men scrubbing at the concrete with a huge bristle brush. I hadn't realised he was there. He had taken off his red uniform jacket and tall black hat and his shirt was filthy. His hair was all over the place and his face was shiny with sweat. Tried to stop my heart from beating so fast – wonder how much he had heard? He didn't seem concerned, just gave us a cheeky grin and apologised. Said he'd got bored of Miss Muffet's story, so had latched on to what we were saying instead.

Decided to go for distracting tactics. 'Let me guess,' I said. 'Is her story about a spider?'

He laughed and said I was a genius, then told us his name was Josh. Started to introduce myself but he already knew who I was! Says he remembers me from Cinders' engagement party!

I felt my face going lava-hot; I couldn't remember him at all. He didn't seem to mind. Just smiled and said there were a lot of new faces that evening – and that All The King's Men all look the same in their uniforms. Then someone called his name, so he had to go – but he said it was great to see me again!

When Josh had gone Bo just squealed, 'Who was that?' She said I'd been flirting with him. Which I absolutely, definitely hadn't.

Totally worth Bo's teasing though, for what happened next. Rapunzel came sauntering over, her stupid silken braid wrapped around her arm, and tried to make me feel small. She made a pathetic comment about Josh telling me to keep away from the TV cameras, so I didn't frighten people watching at home – yeah, ha ha – and then shimmied her way back to Goldilocks, and that's when the heel of one of her fancy gold sandals caught in the cobbles. She fell, totally full length, into a puddle of gooey egg. Even better – Goldilocks rushed over to help, slipped, and ended up beside her in the sticky mess. The sight of the two of them, wailing about the state of their hair and outfits as they sat covered in yolk, was the funniest thing me and Bo had ever seen. I looked over at Josh and caught his eye; he was laughing too.

October 15th

The clean-up is complete and a tree has been planted in the square in honour of Humpty Dumpty. Only a few of The King's Men were there during the last few days, overseeing things. Didn't see Josh again. Not that I was expecting to. Or particularly wanted to. Don't even know why I mentioned him really.

The baking at home is getting more frantic. Mum and Agatha are both in a really bad mood and when The Wicked Queen came round the other day there was a lot of yelling coming from the kitchen. Don't think things are going too well. With any luck, they won't be able to get the potion right and will abandon the whole idea of poisoning Cinderella.

October 18th

Was woken at about 2am by a loud noise coming from downstairs. 'We've done it! We've done it!' Mum and Agatha were shouting. Peered through the banisters and saw them through a crack in the door, jumping up and down and hugging each other. In the middle of the kitchen table sat a red apple glowing eerily in the darkness. Uh-oh.

November

November 2nd

Haven't had time to write for the last couple of weeks because things have taken a sinister turn. As soon as I saw that luminous red apple, I knew it was getting serious. It turns out Mum and Agatha are planning to bake individual apple pies for all the guests, and they're going to use the poisoned apple in Cinderella's! They ordered the fruiterer to bring his reddest apples round to the house and they picked through them all, looking for the brightest and shiniest, so that their poisoned fruit won't look suspicious.

My first thought was to swap the poisoned apple for a normal one and hope that they don't notice, but Mum has the apple locked in her bedside cabinet and there's no way I'll be able to get the key off her.

November 5th

Sat for ages in Bo's bedroom this morning, trying to think of ways to get to the poisoned apple. Bo thinks we should just tell Cinderella. She figures that if someone was planning on poisoning her she'd want to know about it.

I'm not convinced. I don't want to upset Cinderella if I can help it. If Mum and Agatha aren't at the wedding because The King has thrown them in the tower, Cinderella will be devastated. I reckon it's much better to stop the poisoned apple going into the pie in the first place. Then Cinderella will be none the wiser, and Mum and Agatha will just assume that they messed up on the spell.

The only thing now is to figure out how are we going to get the key. Bo and I were trying to come up with something when her mum yelled from downstairs. Bloomin' sheep had got out (again). Guess who ended up giving Bo a hand (again)?

November 6th

We were looking for those stupid sheep for the rest
of the day. By the time I finally got home it was
almost dark. 'See if you can get that key,' I heard
Bo yell as she disappeared over the hill with her
flock. Spent the walk home thinking about how
that was a whole lot easier said than done. Then
things took a turn...

I was sure that dinner time had long gone,
and was expecting the kitchen would be locked
again, so I was surprised to see a light on in there.
The door was ajar and I could hear Mary-Mary
humming quietly. Sauntered into the kitchen to
find her rolling out pastry.

First thought: chance to grab something to eat
before bed, hurrah. Even better news: according
to Mary-Mary, Agatha was out and Mum was in
the bath.

Second thought: so what was Mary-Mary
doing? Hmmm – they'd only managed to rope
her into making some pies for the wedding. Not
another practice batch, either. Mary-Mary said
these pies were actually for the wedding. They

were going into the freezer and coming out the night before.

Took my head out of the fridge (where I was trying to decide if cheese was a bad idea at that time of night). My heart – and mind – were racing. If the pies were being made now, then I might be too late to swap the poisoned apple for another one. Must've looked a bit weird, as Mary-Mary asked if I was okay and said I'd gone very pale.

Sure she thought I was bonkers when I started sorting through the huge basket of apples. I got a bit flustered and they started going everywhere, rolling under the table and oven and making Mary-Mary tut crossly. Said I was hungry so Mary-Mary snapped that I should just take an apple from the top.

'Where's the other one?' I asked, searching frantically through the basket. The apples were all identical; fire-engine red and as shiny as glass. But according to Mary-Mary there were no other apples: those were the only ones she'd been given. She got so frustrated with me that she gave me one of the finished pies from the windowsill, making me promise not to tell Mum.

Brought the pie straight up here to think. What's wrong with me? Of course the poisoned apple wouldn't have been in the basket with the others. Cinderella's pie will have to be baked separately so that she gets the right one (or wrong one, depending on how you look at it), probably on the eve of the wedding. Am going to have a snoop around while Mum's still in the bath.

WOOOOOOOAAAAAAAAAAH! MY HEART IS POUNDING AND MY BREATHING IS DEAFENING. I cannot believe what just happened. I feel sick.

Here's what occurred. Crept outside my room (remembering to leave the apple pie inside – no need to carry around incriminating evidence) to check out the bathroom situation. I could tell by the steam billowing from under the bathroom door that Mum was settled in for the duration. Her clothes and jewellery were draped over the chair outside, and that's when I noticed it hanging from her gold necklace: a tiny key.

I picked up the necklace with shaking hands. I had no way of knowing how long Mum would stay in the bathroom, but surely this was too good an opportunity to pass up. All I would have to do was get rid of the poisoned apple, replace it with one from the basket downstairs, and return the key before Mum noticed it was missing.

Crept into Mum's bedroom. The curtains were drawn, so the room was almost in darkness, but I could make out a pinprick of weirdly glowing light coming from the keyhole of the bedside cabinet drawer: the apple was definitely inside. I took a deep breath to try to calm my nerves and knelt in front of the cabinet. My hands were quivering, making it difficult to fit the key into the lock.

It took about a hundred attempts (well, maybe about 6) but then the key slotted in the tiny hole. That's when I heard Mum call out, 'Mary-Mary, warm me some milk, and bring it to me in bed.'

I could hear the water swirling down the drain. She was out of the bath. I hurriedly turned the key but somehow knocked it out of the lock. It fell on to the wooden floor with a tiny clatter and skidded under the bed. Panicking, I lay flat on the floor and reached for it, just as Mum came in, wrapped in a towel. Her face was thunderous.

Dickory dock! What to say? Had to think fast: I managed to stammer that I'd lost an earring and was checking under all the beds.

'And is it there?' Mum asked. Her voice was dangerously quiet.

Stammered no and she hissed at me to get out, and never come in her room uninvited again. I nodded and scurried past her, with the key clasped in my fist. Mum slammed the door hard behind me. I flung the necklace on to the pile of clothes that were still on the chair outside the bathroom and ran into my bedroom, stepping into the apple pie that was on the floor in the process.

So, here I am. Gingerbread, that was close! Okay. I need a plan B. And some wet wipes for my sticky feet.

November 7th

Phoned Bo first thing this morning. Have taken to sitting on my bed with my chin resting on my knees and rocking gently. Think I'm still traumatised by last night's close call. Bo tried to look on the bright side: at least now I know where she keeps the key, and when she leaves it unattended. So next time she's in the bath I can 'just try again'.

Yeah, right. I swear that girl hasn't listened to a single word I've said. If she had been the one who almost died of a heart attack, then she wouldn't be so relaxed about the situation. Don't think she liked it when I hissed at her: I AM NOT going to do that again. We need to think of something else.

Bo can't meet up today. Sounded down the phone line like she was feeling a bit put out.

Put the phone down and realised that Agatha was lingering in the doorway. Don't know how long she'd been standing there, but she sat on my bed and smirked at me: 'So, what are you "not going to do again"?'

'Look for Bo Peep's sheep,' I said quickly (very proud of my quick thinking these days). 'I'm sick of searching Storybook for them every other day.' I could tell that Agatha didn't believe me; she was looking at me in a way that made me feel really uncomfortable. Then she reached behind me and picked up this very diary. 'Maybe I'll find the real answer to my question in here,' she said, and began to leaf through.

I yelled that it's private and managed to grab it off her. Gingerbread (again! Sorry, my language is getting worse in these stressful times.) I held it to my chest, terrified that she would try to wrestle it from me. Instead, she gave a small smile and put her face close to mine. 'I can wait,' she whispered. Ugh, her breath STINKS.

November 10th

For the last couple of days Agatha has watched me like a hawk, waiting for me to pull my diary from its secret hiding place. Every time I want to write in it, she seems to appear out of nowhere with a hideous smirk plastered across her face. Last night I removed it from the gap under the loose floorboard and have resorted to folding it in half and carrying it around in my pocket all the time. Also, am having to write my entries in the toilet (not while I'm actually going to the toilet, might I add).

November 12th
Caught Agatha lifting the loose floorboard under the bed. Looks like I was just in time.

November 13th
Bo seems to be getting less helpful instead of more so. 'What if we just remove the cabinet from your mum's room?' was her suggestion today.

I looked at Bo with disdain (I know it was with disdain because it's a new word I learnt) and coldly pointed out that I think she might notice that a piece of furniture was missing. Especially the one with her precious apple in it.

Bo shrugged and continued flicking through Weird World Magazine. She read bits out to me: all about something called 'Christmas' that's celebrated in some parts of the world. People exchange presents and bring a tree inside the house and hang things from it. Totally weird. We both agreed on that, at least.

Quite like the sound of it though. It sounds better than birthdays; would be nice to have a day where everyone gets presents. Then Bo turned the page and started going on about sea serpents being spotted off the coast of Mermaid Island. I reached across and grabbed the magazine from her. 'Where did you even get this?' I asked. 'You know it only prints rubbish.'

Apparently, the boy who looks after the sheep left it in the field when he fell asleep under the haystack, so Bo had picked it up. She really does read any old trash. I needed her to concentrate though – I've had another idea.

We make another pie, identical to the others and then, the night before the wedding, sneak into the kitchen and put it in the place of the poisoned pie. That's the only pie that hasn't been made yet; it's being left until the last minute so that it doesn't get mixed up with the others. Mum and Agatha won't want to risk poisoning the wrong person, so they'll have to keep it separate because it looks the same as the other pies.

All we have to do is find the pie that's on its own. I bet they won't even be guarding it. As far as Mum and Agatha will be concerned they'll have got away with it.

Bo did agree it's a pretty brilliant idea –
with the added bonus that Mum and Agatha
will think that they've as good as succeeded.
All we have to do is make a pie that looks
exactly like all the others. Bo wrinkled her nose
at this – she couldn't figure how we were going
to do that.

A-ha! I took the pie that Mary-Mary had
given me from the bottom of my wardrobe. It's
a bit mashed because I stood in it, but it will
give us an idea of the size and the thickness
of pastry, that sort of thing. We're both a bit
worried about the actual baking side of things –
neither of us has ever baked anything in our life.
But how hard can it be?

November 20th

The answer to that question is: really, really,
REALLY hard. After almost a week, we finally
came up with something that resembled pastry.
Bo's mother came home to find us covered from
head-to-toe in flour and her kitchen on fire. We
were banned from setting foot in there again.

We mooched off to sit by Humpty Dumpty's memorial tree. Were gloomily wondering what to do next when a carriage clattered past us. It was Mum and Agatha: so we scooted back to mine to use the kitchen while they were out.

Now we knew how to make pastry it didn't take us long to make a pie. But, as I was about to slide it into the oven, Mary-Mary walked in. I jumped out of my skin; the pie went on to the floor and Bo said a word I've never heard her use before.

Good can come out of bad, though. After making Mary-Mary promise not to tell Mum (I said she'd kill me and Bo murmured 'Possibly literally' which would have been v. funny and witty under different circumstances), Bo turned on the charm a bit and persuaded Mary-Mary to help us make a new pie. She said it was a present for her mum, but it was a surprise so we couldn't make it at her house. Absolute genius. By the end of the day, one perfect apple pie was sitting in Bo's freezer; one perfect apple pie which was identical to the ones sat in the freezer at home. Phew!

November 25th

Can finally breathe a sigh of relief now that the pie is made. All we have to do now is defrost it the night before the wedding, bring it here, and swap it for the poisoned one. Easy. In theory.

November 28th

Have spent the last couple of days in a panic because I couldn't find my diary anywhere. Was angry with myself for not being more careful with it. Finally found it this morning; it had slid down between the sofa cushions. Weird thing is I don't remember having it in the living room.

DECEMBER

December 1st

Have been racking my brains, trying to think how my diary ended up in the living room. I don't think it would have fallen out of my pocket without me realising, and I KNOW I haven't sat on the sofa to write an entry. Have a horrible feeling that Agatha might somehow be involved.

December 2nd

Bo's not convinced. Says it must have just fallen out of my pocket. Then, she stupidly said, 'I don't know why you're so worried about it.'

Dur! Because it's a DIARY. Told her how EVERYTHING is written in it: my original suspicions, my first ideas, our plan and how we carried it out.

Everything. Then she finally got it.

She thinks I'm dense for writing it all down.
Spelt it out to her slowly. I did it. Because. It's.
A. Diary. That's the whole point of having one.
Not sure which bit she doesn't understand.

Valid point from Bo though: how much, if
anything, does Agatha know?

Doesn't bear thinking about.

December 11th

Have spent the last week becoming increasingly
paranoid that Agatha has read my diary. Every
time she looks at me her eyes seem to say, 'I
know how you're going to try to stop us', and I'm
literally jumping at everything she says.

This morning she flopped down on to the sofa
and asked if I was meeting my partner in crime
today. I nearly choked on a mouthful of cereal.
'What crime? We're not trying to stop a crime,'
I spluttered, wiping milk from my PJs. I looked
up at Agatha's amused face. She just smirked
that she was only asking if I was seeing Bo Peep,
that's all.

At this rate, I will be a complete nervous wreck by the wedding.

December 15th

Was woken at 7am by someone banging on the door. Knew who it was and what she wanted before I'd even got out of bed. Bo seemed more frantic than normal. Her voice was all quivery and she kept saying, over and over, that the gate was definitely locked before she went to bed, because she'd double-checked and checked again.

We climbed to the top of Jack and Jill's Hill and looked out over the town. Poor Bo. She thinks someone let her sheep out on purpose. I couldn't imagine a reason why anyone would do such a thing – or who, for that matter. Bo thought maybe The Big Bad Wolf, but I don't reckon it's really his style. He's full of huff and puff but doesn't seem to be much of a stealth worker.

In the distance, I could see All The King's Horses and All The King's Men. Thought maybe they might've seen the sheep, so we set off down the hill to ask.

The King's Men were riding in a field not far from the palace and a couple of them came over to us as we approached. One of them was Josh. He grinned and asked what we were up to. Was trying to find some consonants, as my mouth seemed to be full of vowels, when Bo butted in and explained about her sheep. Josh offered to help look for them.

Bo cheered up and smiled for the first time all morning. Josh smiled back, and then looked at me oddly – he even asked if I was feeling okay. Realised that I was still moving my mouth with no words coming out. I tried to smile like a normal person, but felt my neck and face beginning to burn bright red.

Don't know what was up with me. It's not like I fancy him or anything.

December 16th

Bo rang me last night at about 8pm to say that her and Josh had finally found the sheep and had taken them back to her house. I came home about 5pm because they didn't seem to need me.

Bo kept going on about what a great help Josh was. Apparently, she got upset when the sheep still weren't home and it was getting dark, but Josh had hugged her and said he'd search all night if he had to. 'He was so sweet,' she babbled.

He doesn't sound sweet, he sounds like a bit of a suck-up. Don't know why she doesn't just marry him if she loves him so much. Had a funny feeling in my belly for the rest of the night. Think I must've eaten something dodgy.

December 17th

The more I think about this, the more cross I get. Am so angry with Bo Peep because she barely spoke to me the other day when we were looking for the sheep. She wasn't even bothered when I went home early.

Have decided not to speak to her. (Because she practically ignored me, not because she was getting on so well with Josh, am not bothered about that at all. He can talk to whoever he wants. Don't even like him.)

December 19th

Told Mary-Mary that I was still feeling a bit funny. Strange, it's lasted for days now. Wondered if it was something I ate. Mary-Mary laughed at me. 'It's called jealousy,' she said, 'not my cooking, thank you very much.'

Was sitting at the kitchen table, picking miserably at a piece of toast. Couldn't see what there was to be jealous of. Mary-Mary suggested it was because Bo Peep had the confidence to talk to Josh, and I wished I did too – she seems to think I fancy him.

As if! Can't believe she actually thinks I like Josh. He is pompous and arrogant. Bo Peep called again today, but I told her I'm busy. I told her that if she's bored she should call Josh and hang out with him. She pretended she didn't know what I was going on about.

December 20th

Was lounging on the sofa this morning when Agatha flounced in. Just what I needed. 'Why don't you see your little mate any more?' she smirked at me. 'Had a falling out?'

The best retort I could come up with was, 'Why don't you mind your own business?' Am losing my touch. Luckily, the doorbell rang so I stomped off to answer it and left her smirking away. Grrrr.

I expected to see Bo Peep standing there, so I was surprised when it was Josh. He was all smiles and dimples, as if nothing had happened. Stayed cool and aloof and told him that he'd got the wrong house for Bo Peep, she lives down the lane. Said I thought he'd remember that from the other night when he was being a big hero by finding her sheep.

Tried to shut the door, but the annoying twerp stuck his foot in the way. Then he produced a hamper from behind him and asked if I wanted to join him for a picnic! Ooh, I could kick him! Assumed that Bo Peep had turned him down, so told him that I wasn't about to be anyone's last choice to hang out with, especially not his. And anyway, it was 10am. What sort of person has a picnic at 10am in the morning?

So guess what he said? 'Someone who hasn't had breakfast.' Very good. He's too smart sometimes and I just know he thinks it makes him cuter.

Anyway, decided to go on the picnic, but only because I was quite hungry. Definitely NOT because I like him.

Have to admit, the picnic was pretty amazing: muffins and fresh bread, yogurt, honey, fruit and orange juice. Decided to give him a break. He even gave me the last blueberry muffin as a peace offering. 'Friends?' he asked.

'I'd like that,' I admitted. And I would.

December 21st

Called Bo and told her about picnic with Josh. 'I'm glad you rang me,' she said. 'I thought you were ignoring me or something.'

Don't know how she got that idea.

December 22nd

Met Josh in town for a burger and chips and had a lovely time. I take back all the horrible things I've thought about him; he is, in fact, NOT a smarmy and irritating idiot, but actually an interesting, funny, kind person. Not going to admit that to him, though.

December 23rd

Crikey. Bo looks awful! She turned up here at the crack of dawn, looking like she hadn't had a wink of sleep.

Apparently she hadn't: she'd been sitting up all night, keeping watch over her sheep. She's convinced she saw someone hanging around the other night. She says she didn't get a really good look, but there was definitely someone lurking near the bushes.

I wondered out loud if it could be the same person who let the sheep out. (Personally, I'm not convinced that someone did let the sheep out. It's more than likely that Bo just forgot to shut the gate properly. But she is my friend, so I haven't said that.)

Bo's really not sure. It does seem a bit of a coincidence, though. It doesn't help that her mum's away for a few days: she's gone to the fair with Simple Simon. Tried to point out that Bo can't sit up watching every night. Ended up agreeing to help with the sheep while her mum's away. Tonight I'll watch them while she sleeps.

It's the least I can do after all the help she gave me with the pies.

Spent all day together at Bo's house, just chilling. By early evening she was fast asleep. Sat by her kitchen window, where I had a good view of the sheep, all bright in the moonlight. Didn't see anything suspicious all night.

Good thing really. I don't know what on earth I would have done if I had seen something. Or someone.

December 24th

Another lazy day at Bo's. Told her there was nothing to report from my nightwatch, apart from seeing the cow jump over the moon at about ten past one. Spent ages just watching DVDs and playing Songstar. Such a laugh – I think Old Mother Goose makes a nicer noise than us two with the microphone in our hands.

Threw together some toasties then decided to curl up on the sofa and shut my eyes for a while. Next thing I remember was Bo shaking me awake. I was still lying on the sofa, but the room was in darkness. I could see the clock on the DVD player saying it was midnight.

'Someone's out there,' hissed Bo, in my ear. 'Come and look.'

Suddenly felt very wide awake and very nervous. Peering out of the window, I could see that something had spooked the sheep; they were all bunched up in one corner of the pen and a few were bleating. I looked round at Bo. Her eyes were wide with fright and she was shaking.

I leant closer to the window, straining my eyes in the night. Then I saw it: a shadow, a figure in a long, dark cloak, moving swiftly past the sheep pen and into the trees. I could see the gate swinging open in the breeze. Without thinking, I ran outside and slammed it shut again. I must've been feeling brave or bonkers because I shouted out: 'Who's there? Show yourself!'

I was shaking with fear and thought my legs would give way at any second. There was no reply so Bo dragged me back inside. We both sat up for the rest of the night but the stranger didn't return.

December 25th

Came home this morning at dawn and slept until noon. Kept thinking about who would let Bo's sheep out, and why. It's a total mystery.

I went to the shop in the afternoon to get some milk for Mary-Mary and when I came back there was a little present on the doorstep. On the label it said: Merry Christmas Milly. It's a 'Weird World' after all! Love from Bo Peep xxx

Was a photo of the two of us that Bo's mum had taken, in a silver frame with 'Best Friends' engraved on it. My eyes got all watery. Think it must be hayfever or something.

December 26th

Much debate this morning. Bo was sitting cross-legged on my bedroom floor, scoffing chocolates. She reckons we need to ask someone for help – and her best idea is Josh.

I don't really want to get Josh involved in all of this. Surely he'll have a duty to tell The King? Bo says we should at least ask him to help us keep a look out. I say she should stop eating all the green triangles, because they're my favourites.

She's right, though, it WAS pretty scary the other night. Now, don't get me wrong, I HATE to play the weak, defenceless maiden card, but I guess three pairs of eyes are better than two. And he has a sword.

I'll call him.

December 27th

The three of us watched in shifts last night, but we didn't see anything or anyone. Josh seemed a bit annoyed, and kept asking us if we're sure we saw someone. He must've asked about a million times, and every time Bo and I yelled 'YES!' at him.

It was so frustrating; I'm sure he thought we'd made it up so we could get him alone or something. (As if that would happen – yuk, I still only like him as a friend.)

He wasn't convinced at all. Kept sighing and eventually said that he was going to leave us to it.

Erm, got a bit hysterical and literally shouted 'NO!' Then made it worse: 'There was someone there the other night, creeping around and

acting…creepy.' Heard Bo murmur 'Pathetic'
under her breath. Hope she felt the full effect of
the death look I gave her.

Josh tugged his sleeve away from me (I didn't
even realise I had hold of it; must have got caught
on my bracelet or something) and said he really
had to go. Tried to regain my cool so just said
okay, we didn't need his help anyway.

Knew we could keep watch by ourselves,
really. Have been sitting up for ages writing this
and checking out of the window, but nothing's
happening out there.

A huge crashing sound in the kitchen just woke
me up. Disaster has struck.

Can't believe we both fell asleep. Grabbed a
shepherds' crook from behind the sofa and inched
towards the kitchen door. Pushed it open with the
crook to see sunlight streaming through a broken
window and shards of glass all over the floor. The
kitchen was empty, but the freezer door
was open. I glanced back at Bo and
she pushed past me to look inside.
The pie has gone.

JANUARY

January 3rd

I haven't written since someone broke into Bo's
house and stole the pie. I feel as if I'm constantly
being watched and am suspicious of everyone.
Poor Bo is terrified. She's been in tears since
it happened. She keeps saying she can't
understand who would do this…but it's all too
obvious to me. Of course it's got to be Mum
and Agatha.

I'm convinced that my sister read my diary, in
which case she would know all about the decoy
pie and my plan to stop them poisoning Cinderella
on her wedding day.

I'm also wondering about Mary-Mary. How do I
know she's not in on all this as well? She helped us

to make the pie in the first place and she saw how I reacted when she was making the pies for the wedding. She's not stupid; she could have easily pieced it all together.

Don't want to put Bo through all this again, and I'm not convinced that the pie plan will work now it's no longer a secret. I'm just going to have to tell Cinderella. Might even speak to Josh and ask him to come with me to tell The King; he'll know what to do. I should have done that in the beginning.

January 6th

The wedding is only a few days away and it's been a nightmare trying to get away from Mum and Agatha long enough to sneak off and see Josh. Or even get to the phone. I haven't heard from him since the night the pie was stolen. I'm pretty sure I scared him off (as a friend, of course, not a potential boyfriend) with my embarrassing girly behaviour, but I don't have time to worry about that right now. I need his help.

January 7th

Agatha stopped me as I was leaving to see Josh this morning. She wanted to know where I was going. She just won't leave me alone for a minute at the moment. Tried to shove past her, but she wouldn't budge.

My best comeback was just 'Out'. Great, whatever happened to my super-quick thinking and sharp, snappy responses?

'Going to see your boyfriend?' she taunted. 'Or your little mate with the sheep? I haven't seen her around here in a while. I wonder why that is?'

I saw myself as Agatha must see me: a little girl, a nobody, capable of nothing, and I suddenly felt strong. Strong enough to push her aside, which was totally excellent, seeing her tottering sideways – but also strong enough to take her on in her wicked plan. I am NOT going to let her and Mum get away with it – not without putting up a fight, anyway.

She grabbed my arm and put her face close to mine. 'Be careful, Mildred,' she hissed, warningly. 'Be careful.' Her breath still stinks. She really does

need to make friends with Mr Mouthwash
before she even thinks about getting a boyfriend.

Practically ran to Josh's house. My arm was
throbbing where Agatha held it so tightly and
I had to keep sniffing and blinking away tears.
I was banging on the door for ages before Josh
finally answered, and when he did I practically
flung myself at him. Looking back, I'm ashamed
to even think about it. I think I'd got so worked
up by that stage that I was sobbing and gulping
like a little baby.

I told him the whole unfortunate story.
Obviously, it took a while for him to get his head
around it. First, he couldn't grasp the idea of a
poison apple in a pie. Then he struggled with
the concept that Bo and I had made a bogus pie
to try to thwart their plan. Then he looked a bit
disbelieving that someone had broken into Bo's
house to steal the pie from the freezer.

I tried to get him to grasp the seriousness of the
situation. He couldn't see that it was too much
of a coincidence for someone to know what they
were looking for, and where, and that someone

prepared to poison Cinderella was probably happy to do serious stuff to keep me and Bo out of the way. So I really needed him to say he'd come with me to tell The King all about it.

Josh put his hand on my shoulder and looked at me, his face full of concern. 'Are you sure you're not just over-tired?' he said, softly and slowly like I was an idiot.

AAAAAAAAAAGGGGGGGGGGH! He so wasn't listening – why wouldn't he believe me?

Then we were interrupted by a massive banging on the door. I could hear Bo shouting. Josh opened the door and she rushed in, completely out of breath. I haven't heard from her in days – why did she choose now to pop up, right in the middle of me trying to make Josh see sense? Not that I minded anyone else being there with me and him, of course. It's not like we wanted to spend time on our own together.

Anyway, turns out the reason she'd gate-crashed was to tell us some news. News that Josh could've told me. Apparently, it's too late to tell The King about the poisoning plot.

They've all gone away. Josh looked at Bo and then at me, and maybe started to figure that I'd actually been telling the truth.

'I'm afraid she's right,' he gulped. 'The whole family have gone away until the wedding. It's sort of a tradition.'

Deep breaths. Now we'll just have to find another way to stop them.

January 8th

Here's our plan. Bo and Josh are coming round soon to help me. We're going to wait until Mum and Agatha have gone to bed, then I'm going to creep into the kitchen, find the poisoned pie, and put one of the others in its place. If they're a pie short at the wedding, it's no big deal. (Peter Peter Pumpkin Eater is going to be there and there's no way he'll eat apples.) Bo will wait in the bushes outside the window for me to pass her the pie. Josh is going to keep watch for anyone coming; if it looks like there's going to be trouble, he can go and get the rest of The King's Men. It'd better work.

Not taking any chances with my diary this time. I've got a new jacket with an inside pocket that's the perfect size to keep my diary and pen in. It would be fatal (literally! Yikes, that scares me just thinking about it) if the wrong person found out about our plans this time.

Bo and Josh have just arrived. Bo looks scared witless. Josh looks quite handsome. Must be because it's nearly dark. He squeezed my hand when he came in and asked if I was okay. I felt my belly flip over. (Obviously nerves.)

Now it's just a waiting game.

January 9th

All The King's Horses and All The King's Men aren't going to be able to get me out of this one. We're stuffed. I'm in Rapunzel's Tower, about a million feet up in the air (okay, that's a bit of an exaggeration – but you get the idea). Feels like it's swaying in the breeze, but that could be something to do with the massive bump on my head.

Oh, gingerbread, I can hardly bear to write down what happened. Waited until all the lights had gone out last night and we were sure that Mum and Agatha had gone to bed, then I crept into the kitchen. It all seemed okay: the room was silent except for the tick-tock of the clock on the wall. The pies were laid out on the countertop; one sitting separately from the rest. As I reached for the pie, I didn't hear someone approaching me from behind. Turns out that it was Agatha, armed with a rolling pin – and she wasn't afraid to use it. My head is still throbbing.

Woke up this morning and it all came flooding back to me. I shouted for what seemed like hours, but there was no one around. I managed to untie my hands and feet pretty quickly (Agatha can't tie knots with those great big sausage fingers of hers), but escaping isn't going to be so easy. I don't know how they got me up here – a spell probably, the little cheats. There's no door, and just one tiny window. My hair only just reaches to the sill, I've already thought of that one.

Glad I've got my diary with me. There's not

much else to do up here except gaze out of the window and feel angry that I can't do anything to help Cinderella. From the window I can see the tops of trees, and in the distance the palace turrets, tinged with pink earlier as the sun began to rise. It looks as if I could reach out with my hand and touch it. I keep willing myself not to cry, but it's so difficult. I keep thinking about the wedding, and about my friends: what's happened to them? Are they trapped somewhere? Are they hurt? Are they coming to rescue me? Do they even know I'm here?

Am making a mess of my page with tears splashing on to my writing. Feel awful from crying so much (and being mashed on the head probably didn't help either). Not sure about seeing stars, but I do feel like I might be hearing things. Sounds like someone calling my name over and over. Sounds like Josh. Mustn't ever confess that to him, or he'll think I've started dreaming about him.

Hang on a minute: it IS Josh! Outside the tower, here, now!

January 10th

Okay, so we've a lot of catching up to do here.
Things have moved on pretty fast and changed
drastically. First of all, it really was Josh outside
the tower – I wasn't having strange ideas from
my knock on the head.

He'd brought with him All The King's Horses
and All The King's Men, and they stretched out
a huge blanket beneath the window for me to
jump on to. Yeah, right! But I didn't really have
much of a choice, did I? And it kind of helped that
Josh was standing right next to it, calling out
words of encouragement.

I closed my eyes, took a deep breath, and
jumped. It was truly terrifying – which I think is
the perfect justification for clinging on to Josh
as he helped me clamber off the blanket. Then I
thought about Bo. My legs felt like jelly, but I was
really worried that Bo might be in danger. Josh
assured me she was fine – she was on her way to
the palace to try to stop Mum and Agatha from
getting there.

Josh was really looking after me. He was keen to take me to Doctor Foster to get my bump checked out, even though I kept saying I was fine. As it turns out, Doctor Foster had gone to Gloucester, so Josh agreed to leave it. He helped me up on to his horse and we raced off to find Bo.

When we got back to Storybook, the village was deserted. Everyone was at the wedding – except for a very bedraggled looking Bo Peep, sitting by the side of the road on Little Miss Muffet's Tuffet. It turns out that she had decided to block the road to the palace with her flock of sheep, so that Mum and Agatha couldn't get their carriage through.

It was a good plan, but things went wrong when The Big Bad Wolf came along. All the sheep got frightened and ran away, and although Bo tried to block the carriage herself, they just mowed her down. Poor Bo, she looked like she needed a big hug, but she told us not to bother about her right then. Sure enough, we were running out of time. Josh dragged her up on to the horse's back too – good job she's only Little Bo Peep not Supersize Me Bo Peep.

We galloped through the village square on our way to the palace. I could see the clock tower; there was a loud 'DONG', and I saw the mouse running down the side.

'The clock struck one!' I shouted into Josh's ear, and he spurred his horse on faster.

I kept saying, over and over to myself, please don't let us be late. I couldn't bear the thought of Mum and Agatha winning, of Cinderella's chance of a better life being snatched away because of their jealousy and evil.

We stopped in front of the palace gates. Josh, Bo and I dismounted and approached the guard, who wondered what the heck was going on. I explained that I'm Cinderella's stepsister and that we were all late for the wedding. He looked at my mud-spattered clothes and Bo's dishevelled hair, narrowed his eyes, and his lip curled. 'Well, I can certainly believe that you're one of The Ugly Sisters,' he said to me. I should've been cross – a few months ago, a comment like that would have just confirmed why I hated everyone – but I could kind of see where he was coming from.

'HEY!' shouted Josh, and he grabbed the guard by his shirt. Wow! I calmed him down and pleaded with the guard to let us in. It was, after all, truly a matter of life and death. The guard eventually opened the gate, rolling his eyes – and then informed us that the wedding ceremony was over and that everyone was now seated in the banqueting hall.

I rushed past the guard, with Bo and Josh close behind me. My legs were burning and I felt as if I would collapse at any second, but somehow I made it to the door and heaved it open. Silence. The palace was deserted. We dashed across the slippery marble floor as quickly as we could, heading for the large double doors of the banqueting hall.

Everyone turned to stare at us as we walked in; Mary-Mary, Jack and Jill, The Butcher, The Baker, The Candlestick Maker and every other resident of Storybook. They were all seated at little round tables adorned with red and gold centrepieces and velvet tablecloths. At the far end of the room sat Cinderella and The Handsome Prince and beside them, The King, Mum and Agatha. Agatha saw me and clapped her hand to her mouth in shock.

Cinders saw me and waved me over. She was trying to get the waiters to bring me some food when I saw The Handsome Prince lean towards her. I glanced at the silver plate in front of her. On it was a piece of untouched pie, the filling glowing ominously red. The Handsome Prince took his spoon and scooped up a chunk of the poisoned pie, and I was close enough to hear him say, 'Try this, darling,' as he held the spoon to Cinderella's lips. 'It's delicious.'

Suddenly, everything seemed to go in slow motion; the guests clapping and laughing, the blush creeping across Cinderella's cheeks, Mum and Agatha's evil smiles. Before I even knew what I was doing, I found myself waving my arms and shrieking like a loony. I leapt across the table, pushing Cinderella to the ground. Glasses and plates went flying and smashed on the floor. I remember hearing everyone in the room gasp. The spoon that was just inches away from Cinderella's lips found its way into mine instead and I felt a numb, tingling sensation in my mouth that spread to the rest of my head, then to my chest and the rest of my body.

Breathing was difficult. I couldn't see. I heard Bo and Josh shouting my name, their voices a thousand miles away, as I fell to the ground.

Obviously, the next bit is what Bo has told me since. Even more obviously, I didn't die. But why? Because I hadn't had love's first kiss – obviously!

'Honestly, it's the most romantic thing I've ever seen,' Bo gushed this morning, as she sat by my bed. Doctor Foster has prescribed complete bed-rest for the next couple of days. (Luckily he came back from Gloucester early after a torrential downpour caused him to step into a puddle right up to his middle. He's sworn he's never going there again.)

Apparently, after I 'died', Josh practically flew over the tables to get to me and held me in his arms and, Bo says, he was crying! I've made boys cry before but not for the right reasons.

'He told you that you were the most beautiful person he'd ever known,' said Bo. I kind of liked hearing about it, but it made me blush big time. She was just telling me that he kissed me – the sweetest, loveliest kiss you can imagine – when Josh himself appeared in my bedroom doorway, holding a MASSIVE bunch of flowers.

After trying to find out who gave the sweetest, loveliest kisses, Josh sat at the end of my bed and grinned at me. Bo disappeared pronto – she's about as subtle as a wrecking ball. I sat up to say thank you to Josh (made my head v. woozy) for saving my life. Bless him, he said that I was the one that had saved a life – and then he moved towards me. I think he might have been going to kiss me, but I don't know for sure because I passed out. Typical.

FEBRUARY

february 5th

Mum and Agatha were sentenced today; six months' community service at The Hansel and Gretel Foundation for Lost Children. I wasn't in court, but Bo said they cried like babies when they heard. It's the worst punishment they could have received: having to work selflessly for others.

Bo was really cross. She thinks they should have locked them in a dungeon and thrown away the key. I tried to point out that they would only have sat and plotted more evil things. Even if they weren't able to carry them out, the evil thoughts would have been there. This way, their minds are going to be occupied with doing good. Bo can't believe I don't hate them – but it's not really their fault. They can't help the way they're written.

We've been moving boxes into our new home. It's well exciting! The Woodcutter is letting us rent his cottage in the woods. It's been empty since Snow White and The Seven Dwarves signed their record deal, so he's glad to have it taken off his hands and isn't charging us too much.

Things are going nicely with Josh; we've gone to the cinema a few times and we had dinner with Cinderella and The Handsome Prince the other night. He turned up today, just in time to help us with the heavy stuff.

Cinderella came round earlier, too, with a big bunch of flowers. She wanted to know where Josh was – turns out she had something to ask me while he wasn't there. She only went and asked if there'll be wedding bells for us two soon!

Erm, I don't think so. At least, not until I've done all the things I've always wanted to do but never had the confidence to: learn to drive a carriage, go to that new nightclub in town, have a girls' holiday abroad (Jill and Sleeping Beauty said they're up for it). Then we'll see. But it's early days yet.

february 10th

Today I received a medal for bravery! I was presented with it by The King in the town square. I felt so proud, especially when the crowd cheered; Bo and Josh were the loudest, of course.

As I stepped down from the platform, Goldilocks and Rapunzel sloped up. Rapunzel seemed jealous – said the whole town's talking about me. I felt quite shy again, she wanted to know how it feels to be a celebrity! Then Goldilocks piped up: 'And what exactly is the deal with Josh?' She honestly sounded WELL jealous.

Before I could answer, Josh came through the crowd and picked me up. He spun me round and round and said he's so proud of me. Then the best thing happened: Rapunzel put her arm on Josh's and asked if we'd like to go to her party on Saturday night. She was really rude to Bo – she glanced in her direction and said it was only a small party, not many people were invited. Like Bo would want to go, anyway. But Josh just stepped away from her and said – wait for it – 'No thanks, my girlfriend and I have plans with our friend Bo Peep.'

YESSSSSSSSSS! And then we waltzed off into the congratulating crowd, leaving the two of them open-mouthed behind us.

february 20th

Flicking through this diary, I've noticed how few and far between my entries have been recently. My life is just so full at the moment, I haven't had the time to write. Bo and I have made the cottage really homely and we're getting on great as housemates (despite the fact that she always leaves empty pizza boxes on the kitchen work surface, and never does the washing up).

We recently sold our story to the Storybook Times, and since then have been inundated with people wanting us to solve crimes for them. Bo sold her sheep to Old MacDonald and, along with the money from the newspaper story, we rented some office space in town and have set up a Private Investigators company: Milly Peeps. It's early days, but we're getting there.

At the moment we're working with The Three Little Pigs, investigating a recent spate of houses being blown down. I'm expecting a breakthrough any day now...

THE END

Are YOU a fairytale villain?

Discover whether you're a porridge-eating trespasser, or a glass-slipper-wearing do-gooder.

1 Surprise, surprise, Jack and Jill have fallen down the hill (again). Do you:
   a. Fetch the vinegar and brown paper
   b. Send for Doctor Foster
   c. Call All The King's Men (any excuse!)
   d. Leave them, it's their own fault for trying to carry all that water

2 Rapunzel has got her hair caught in a drain. Do you:
   a. Lend her a hand, and a pair of scissors
   b. Ask her to be nicer to you, and dangle her hair in dirty drain water if she refuses
   c. Help her (in return for her best necklace)
   d. Laugh – serves her right for being so stuck up

3 You spot Agatha skiving off from her community service. Do you:
  a. Promise not to tell, as long as she makes up with Milly and does three good deeds
  b. Ask Josh and All The King's Men to 'arrest' her, until she learns her lesson
  C. Tell her mum – she'll jump at the chance to dream up a really nasty punishment
  d. Lock her in the tower and leave her there for a day, or three

4 You've been invited to the Royal Garden Party, but your best friend hasn't. Do you:
  a. Hand her your ticket, with a winning smile, and tell her to have a wonderful time
  b. Try to sneak the both of you in without getting caught
  C. Ask for another invite, but if you can't get one, go anyway – it's the party of the year
  d. Start planning your outfit, she'll get over it

Quiz answers

Add up your score to find out where you are on the fairytale villain scale.

A = 4, B = 3, C = 2, D = 1

15-16 Goodie~goodie - Cinderella
You're a real goodie, erm, one shoe, and it sort of makes everyone a little bit, well...sick.

11-14 Not bad - Tinkerbell
Your intentions are good, in their own way, but you're just a bit too mischievous to pull it off as a goodie.

7-10 Could be worse - Goldilocks
Okay, so you stole some porridge, but you promise you'll never do it again. (Probably.)

4-6 Baddie - Wicked Queen
Ouch, villain alert!
And no, I don't want an apple thank you very much.

Profile of a fairytale villain

Milly Peeps keeps a profile of each Storybook resident. Here's a sneaky glimpse...

Character:	Wicked Queen
Age:	38, masquerading as 29
Status:	Not the fairest of them all? We'll see about that...
Interests:	Looking in the mirror, pampering oneself, shopping
Music:	*Ring a Ring o' Roses* (the best bit's where they all fall down)
Baddie factor:	Big Bad levels of badness
Signature dish:	Poison apple, like toffee apple but with a twist
Arch-enemy:	Snow White, of course, pay attention!
Partner in crime:	Your trusty mirror-mirror upon the wall. He may be two-faced, but he's always right there when you need him.

How to make a delicious apple pie (without killing anybody)

Here's a delicious, poison-free apple pie recipe to delight your friends with.

Ingredients
for the pastry

255g/9oz plain flour
140g/5oz margarine
  or butter
6 tsp cold water
Pinch of salt

for the filling

3 large Bramley cooking apples (non-poisonous), chopped, stewed and cooled, with sugar added to taste.

REMEMBER! ALWAYS ASK AN ADULT TO HELP YOU WHEN USING THE OVEN!

Method

Preheat oven to 200°C/400°F/Gas 6.

1. Sift the flour and salt into a bowl.
2. Rub in the margarine or butter until the mixture resembles fine breadcrumbs.
3. Add the cold water to the mixture. Using a knife, mix the water into the flour, using your hand to

firm up the mixture. The pastry should be an even colour and a suitable consistency for rolling.

4. Divide the pastry in half. Roll one half out so that it's big enough to cover a 20cm/8in baking dish. Carefully trim away any excess pastry, using the edge of the dish as your guide.

5. Pour the stewed apples into the pastry case.

6. Roll out the other half of the pastry and place it on top. Use milk to moisten the edges, and press them down until sealed.

7. Carefully trim off any excess pastry and flute the edges using a pinching action.

8. Prick the top of the pie and bake in the oven for 20–30 minutes.

Dust your poison-free pie with caster sugar and serve to your friends!

Watch out for:
The Big Bad(ish) Wolf

Another fairytale villain gets to tell his
side of the story, in his own private diary.
Balthazar J Wolf is not so much bad as...
well...misunderstood. Find out how he tries
to redeem his reputation by helping The
Three Little Pigs, confronting a giant troll
and trying to become a vegetarian.